D0459147

NO LONGER PROPERTY OF
ANYTHINK LIBRARIES/
RANGEVIEW LIBRARY DISTRICT

WRITTEN BY
KATHY Z. PRICE

ILLUSTRATED BY
CARL JOE WILLIAMS

MARDI GRAS

Atheneum Books for Young Readers
New York London Toronto Sydney New Delhi

ALMOST DIDN'T COME THIS YEAR

ACKNOWLEDGMENTS

The author wishes to express deep gratitude to the vibrant members of the New Orleans diaspora, the residents, Katrina survivors, family, city officials, and all who contributed to this book: Yvonne Recastner Payne, Keith Clayton, Charisse Davis, Courtney Lott, Janet Rochon—thank you a million times. Special thanks to Mayor LaToya Cantrell, honorable Councilman Jay Banks, and Inez Pierre of Crescent City Floats. *Laissez les bons temps rouler.*

Ⱥ ATHENEUM BOOKS FOR YOUNG READERS • An imprint of Simon & Schuster Children's Publishing Division • 1230 Avenue of the Americas, New York, New York 10020 • Text © 2022 by Kathy Z. Price • Illustration © 2022 by Carl Joe Williams • Book design © 2022 by Simon & Schuster, Inc. • All rights reserved, including the right of reproduction in whole or in part in any form. • ATHENEUM BOOKS FOR YOUNG READERS is a registered trademark of Simon & Schuster, Inc. Atheneum logo is a trademark of Simon & Schuster, Inc. • For information about special discounts for bulk purchases, please contact Simon & Schuster Special Sales at 1-866-506-1949 or business@simonandschuster.com. • The Simon & Schuster Speakers Bureau can bring authors to your live event. For more information or to book an event, contact the Simon & Schuster Speakers Bureau at 1-866-248-3049 or visit our website at www.simonspeakers.com. • The text for this book was set in Avallon, Bellfort Rough Demo, Brandon Grotesque, & News Gothic. • The illustrations for this book were rendered mixed media, painting, and collage on paper. • Manufactured in China • 1121 SCP • First Edition • 10 9 8 7 6 5 4 3 2 1 • Library of Congress Cataloging-in-Publication Data • Names: Price, Kathy (Kathy Z.), 1957- author. | Williams, Carl Joe, illustrator. • Title: Mardi Gras almost didn't come this year / Kathy Z. Price ; illustrated Carl Joe Williams. • Other titles: Mardi Gras almost did not come this year • Description: First edition. | New York : Atheneum, [2022] | Summary: Lala, Babyboy, and their parents struggle to cope with the loss of their home to Hurricane Katrina, but find joy again in the celebration of Mardi Gras. • Includes facts about Hurricane Katrina and glossary. • Identifiers: LCCN 2018046686| ISBN 9781534444256 (hardcover) | ISBN 9781534444263 (ebook) • Subjects: | CYAC: Loss (Psychology)—Fiction. | Family life—Louisiana—Fiction. | Hurricane Katrina, 2005—Fiction. | Mardi Gras—Fiction. | Louisiana—Fiction. • Classification: LCC PZ.7.P9306 Mar 2020 | DDC [E]—dc23 LC record available at https://lccn.loc.gov/2018046686

For Lala (Dolores) Rucker,
Mardi Gras historian Yvonne Payne,
and the courageous people of NOLA, especially the 9th Ward,
who walk the Second Line as prayer in the aftermath. —K. Z. P.

Thanks to the Robinson family, especially Noa, whose love of books fueled my vision of the story.
To Neesa, for her love and support. To Joseph, my son, for his support and feedback.—C. J. W.

Days before the storm,
there was a burning-up sun.

Then,

throwaway corncob days were done,
and the Double Dutch and "Da Doo Ron Ron"
and bebop, which once rocked porches,
banished.

Wind threw Water into Sky,
snatched the Blue out.
Blue sputtered, then died.

The levees cried.

St. Bernard Parish and the Lower Ninth Ward—
vanished.
The cyclone overturned trucks and trees.
Water flooded the land
and destroyed our Trumpet House,
built by our father, a music man.

Me and Babyboy held Mamma
and Pop-Pop tight. We found
Aunt Henny Peck's old shotgun house that night—she moved to Georgia to be with
Sonya and baby Harry. We've been living there since.

Before the storm, Mamma
would say, *It's all right,
Babyboy-baby, Lala-love-lady.*

But it's been
August
September
October
November
December
January

and now it's February.

St. Charles Avenue to Canal, it's almost Blues-day, Fat Tuesday—
truck parades,
a thousand beignets, sweet bakes, King Cakes;
New Orleans one long Mardi Gras mile.

We bought Mamma a nickel of boiled peanuts,
fried jelly beans in a pile,
make mustache faces with string beans and shoelaces,
but why won't Mamma smile?

Our old sweet gum tree still drops her star-shaped leaves each time we visit.
The burned-rubber tire swing pivots.

The Trumpet House sways, buckling, rickety on quick-made stilts.
Waiting to be rebuilt.
But Pop-Pop says, "Rebuilding costs too much money right now."

I sure miss reaching out my window for a persimmon, sun-warmed,
right from the tree; or curling up in the Question Mark branch,
legs swinging free on a hot day or cold.

And I miss Babyboy standing next to that trumpet, pretending to blow.
I'm homesick for Trumpet House every day, 'cause Aunt Henny Peck's
shotgun house is just not the same.

We sit on the steps, waiting for Mamma to return from the store
and Pop-Pop from work. Neighbor Stan-Man blows up purple balloons on his porch.

One gets away, **SSSSSS-ZHHHHHH-OOOOOOO**, flies sky-high with a **POP!**

My brother backward-bops,
"Lala, look a-yonder."
He pokes five fingers up at the sky, bounds off the step—
sneakers fly.
"See that trumpet, go-by, go-by!"
"Babyboy." I pull him down to earth. "Shush, boy, nothing there but clouds."

But Babyboy's feet itch to dance. He squats, bop-to-bop . . .

"Stop," Mamma says. "Won't you please stand tall?"
And she once was the best dance of all.
She walks up the steps, grocery bags in her arms, no carnival charms.
I know, because I peeked—no King Cake, no Mardi Gras beads.

Cicadas echo through the slash pine and magnolia trees.

Babyboy taps the drum on his knees, chanting, "Down down baby, down by the roller coaster, shimmy, shimmy ko-ko-bop."

Mamma frowns, and he stops (but only for a minute).

That zany beat in our feet is 'cause of Pop-Pop, our pa. He sure loved himself some Mardi Gras!

"There are four seasons of the year," he'd declare. "There's Mardi Gras, and Mardi Gras,
and Mardi Gras, and *more* Mardi Gras." Counting each one off on his odd-looking fingertips,
shaped like small drums.

"It's Mardi Gras weather!" he'd shout out whenever, blaring his horn, tilting it high.
Mamma'd laugh till she cried. Hands on hips, she'd sashay barefoot—
the most fancy-dancy of the ball.

"We dance it *old-school*; back, back to the boogaloo, y'all," Pop-Pop would sing out,
twirling his trumpet, blasting his call. "And Mamma is New Orleans's best dance of all."

But Pop-Pop hasn't played his horn, not since the storm.

I shush Babyboy, "Quiet. Can't you see Mamma's cross?"
He scoots off, slams the door . . .

comes right back with Pop-Pop's horn.

"Boy! Give that back!"
 I snatch. He ducks, zigzags the trumpet out of reach.
"Triple bop three. Gal, you ain't the boss of me!"
"Put down that horn, for sassafras's sake," snaps Mamma.
"Go outside."

Babyboy whispers, "But it's Mardi Gras weather."
I take his hand. "No, it's not," I tell him. "It's not coming, ever."
We walk the blocks to our old yard. Sometimes it's hard—
the smell of rotting water;
houses that once stood proud, bowed under decaying wood
or disappeared. Whole streets caved in, ragged ghost avenues.
Just like Mardi Gras and our Trumpet House.

I hold my brother in my lap underneath our whispering sweet gum.

He tap-taps his knees-drum, softly, **TT-T-TAH-TAH-TAH**.

"Babyboy, remember last Mardi Gras? You was King and I was Queen

and you cut the fool at the second-line band. Bang! Bang! You banged on that can."

His face next to mine grows wet.

Mine does too.

That night, I dream the storm comes again,
our red Trumpet House spiraling in the wind.
Then suddenly the wind is quiet;
no more floodwater.

I'm standing on our tire swing,
Babyboy on the other side.
He asks me to sing.

I open my mouth;
nothing rings out, sound stuck
between throat and heaven.

But then I'm hopscotching over Carnival crowns,
pitching doubloons for jacks in onesies and twosies
over Aunt Henny Peck's black-eyed Susies.
Suddenly there's more doubloons,
and purple beads and golden rings
fall out of the sky like rain.
Babyboy watches from the windowpane.

Next morning I know what to do.
It's gonna be Mardi Gras for my little brother.

I sneak out of the closet Babyboy's bang-can drum, his King crown, my tiara and gown. I pull out umbrellas for the second-line jamboree, twirl the red taffeta, high-stepping. **OOOOH-WHEEE!** Me and Babyboy gonna have a blast!

But Mamma catches me,
her eyes pinch,
and she sighs.
"Lala, not so fast. . . ."

When in struts Pop-Pop. . . .

His hands are filled with the palest butter-colored flowers.
"A Mardi Gras present! Prettiest calla lilies in the world,
for the two most beautiful girls."

Mamma takes the bouquet.
Her eyes un-pinch, un-squinch, the teeniest bit.
She touches a flower, and lifts
and lifts
them up in the air to release the scent.
I tuck one bloom in my hair.

And here's another surprise for Babyboy and me to share:
flower bulbs and vegetable seeds.
"These are to plant," Pop-Pop says, "come this spring.
They'll welcome our house, when it's ready."

Just then a **BLAAAAAAST** pierces the morn!

IT'S BABY BOY! ON POP-POP'S HORN
"IT'S MARDI GRAS WEATHER!"
The trumpet blares, easy-peasy pieeeeeeee, in perfect Mardi Gras style.

WHO DAT? WHO DAT? WHO DAT BE?

It's Babyboy—say whaa-at?

MAMMA! BABYBOY can PLAY!

What you say?

YOU LEARN THAT TRUMPET?
ON THE SLY
Who What Where When How & Why
WHAA-AAT!
Git on wit your bad self, Son.
PLAY THAT BOP.

SURE THING, POP-POP!

What that you say—what that you said?

EEEEEEEERRRRRRRRRRRRRRRRRRRRRRRRRRREEEK

How dat TRUMPET SPEAK

TRUMPET SWEET AS JELLY BREAD—

PLAY it, Babyboy!

You SAY it, Babyboy.

Will you WAIL it, Babyboy

FOR YOU MAMMA-MÈRE

Past all Mardi Gras miles

AND JUST LIKE THAT

Ratta bom boom bat—

FINALLY . . .

MAMMA SMILES.

"ALLIGATOR TAIL IN A PO'BOY BUN!" the street vendor cries.
Mardi party's begun!
Babyboy throws the door open wide—all of us, barefoot, run outside.

Jazz stirs Bourbon Street with tremendous shouts,
boiled the bayou, and jumped the kudzu, kudzuing about;
it riled crawfish singing crawfish songs and
bully bullfrogs in their bully frog bogs.

BEEEEEEEEEEEEEEE BOP! Bully frogs hop!
Sing so sweet—*knee-deep-kneeeeeeeeeeeee-deep.*

"Watermelon red to rind," the fruit man sings.
We sniff the sizzle of barbecue wings.
"Lemonade made in shade!"

St. Charles Avenue loves the parade. It's the
Krewe of Muses! Now here come the Zulus, too!
Sunlight snatches back the jazzing blue.
From way-way high, doubloons fall from clouds
like rain.

"Boy, give *me* that trumpet!"
Pop-Pop tilts it high, blows loud as he can—our music man.

"Here it comes! It's the second-line band! Go on, Babyboy, bang on a can!"
Mamma twirls our arms over our heads; she twists, and dips, and heel-toe tips.
Pop-Pop shouts, "Let's dance it old-school."
He sounds the trumpet call.
We bop-to-bop, taller than tall.
I belt out a song, loud and long, longer than a Juney bug's crawl.

"BOOGALOO, BABY, BOOGALOO, Y'ALL!"

Then each one of us sees it, up-up high—
a trumpet cloud gliding
go-by, go-by.
Palms raise up in prayer to the sky.

One day our Trumpet House will be rebuilt—persimmons, Question Mark branch, and all.
Under the sweet gum, the star leaves will fall. But for now,

I am the Queen,
and you are the King,

and Mamma,
New Orleans's best dance of all.

AUTHOR'S STORY:

I was just about Lala's age when my brothers and sister and I visited my cousins in New Orleans for the first time. Their home, so different from the California ranch house I grew up in, seemed like magic to me: huge oak trees to peek around for hide-and-seek, pecans falling right from the branches, grasshoppers with wild screechy sounds (my cousins said they were cicadas). My mother, Helen, and my aunts Yvonne and Katherine bought out the local seafood market and lugged home buckets of live crab, giant shrimp, and a million crawfish for a gigantic pot of tasty Creole gumbo. And of course, there was boogaloo and blues music turned up loud as it could go on the stereo, with us kids showing off the latest dance moves. My cousins pulled out gold coins and sparkly beads from something they called *Mardi Gras*. They told us it came once a year and we'd missed it. But they shared generously, giving us Mardi Gras souvenirs to take home. We visited New Orleans again, but somehow, we always seemed to miss the big Mardi Gras.

NEW ORLEANS COUNCILMAN JAY BANKS'S ZULU PORCH FLOAT *(ABOVE AND RIGHT)*

HURRICANE KATRINA

"Imagine New Orleans as a punch bowl, with the Mississippi River on one side and a lake on the other, waiting to fill that bowl up. Somewhere between Saturday and Sunday, two hundred miles from the eye of the storm, we braced ourselves," my cousin Keith Clayton said. He was a first responder as well as NOLA resident. He went on: "When the levees exploded, it sounded like a cannon firing. The most destructive force was the sheer volume and power of water." My cousin lost everything and had to wait a year for his house to be rebuilt. Some families are still waiting.

"Close your eyes," says ex-King of the Zulu Krewe, and now New Orleans's official Councilman Jay Banks.

"Picture your neighborhood grocery store, where you get your hair cut, favorite playground, your best friend's house. Do you see it? Now open your eyes.

"Everything is gone."

AFTER KATRINA: MARDI GRAS

I knew I wanted to write about New Orleans and the children who lived through Hurricane Katrina. During school visits I met children—like Lala and Babyboy—whose families were forced to relocate, sometimes to other parts of New Orleans, sometimes as far away as New York, Georgia, and California. These courageous children were the reason I wrote this story. Lala and Babyboy's Trumpet House was inspired by houses of New Orleans musicians such as the late Fats Domino, an African American pianist and singer-songwriter. He was a NOLA resident; his house, destroyed by Katrina was rebuilt.

I asked Councilman Banks to share the one moment that meant the most after the storm:

"Normal, as we knew it, was gone, but NOLA pulled together as a community. There were people who could not get to their houses; my own house was at the bottom of the punch bowl, I didn't see it for three weeks. But everybody RIGHT THERE, busy helping others regain their homes, even though they didn't have their own—that was our proudest moment.

"I grew up with Mardi Gras in my DNA," Councilman Banks said. "There is nothing like a Cypress tree, we are resilient, and we, the people of New Orleans, throw the *best* party in the entire *world*."

Then Councilman Banks said something else, in French:

"LAISSEZ LES BONS TEMPS ROULER, LAISSEZ LES BONS TEMPS ROULER."

"What does that mean?" I asked.

"LET THE GOOD TIMES ROLL, LET THE GOOD TIMES ROLL."

MARDI GRAS AND COVID-19

Just as Lala and Babyboy worried that Mardi Gras would not come because of Hurricane Katrina, citizens in New Orleans wondered *again*, with Covid-19 and social distancing precautions for public health, *Would Mardi Gras come THIS year?* Mardi Gras, also known as "Fat Tuesday," is the biggest celebration day before Ash Wednesday, the start of a forty-day solemn religious observance.

Mardi Gras is always a part of that religious observance, but parades were shut down during the pandemic. "At first, we were very sad," said Inez Pierre of Crescent City Floats. "Everyone plays parade. That's what you do in NOLA. You pretend you are in a marching band. Making the floats is our business and we look forward to Mardi Gras more than other holidays. But then, we thought of porch floats! And suddenly we had MORE business than ever. Everybody wanted to celebrate Mardi Gras with a porch float, and this was a safe way to have a Mardi Gras celebration."

"What we knew is that we couldn't do Mardi Gras the way we used to with this pandemic raging," Councilman Banks said. "That was a certainty."

AFTER THE STORM

Storms show you how vulnerable you can be. After experiencing New Orleans at the very worst, my cousin Keith told me, "If you still live here, after all NOLA has been through, that means you really want to be here."

I visited New Orleans after Hurricane Katrina, on a Greyhound bus. On arrival, the driver announced. "THIS . . . is New Orleans." He said this proudly, as if he were introducing his absolute best friend.

As I walked down the steps of the bus into the city, I, too, felt like New Orleans was my good friend. And not only a good friend; I felt New Orleans was my family.

GLOSSARY

Alligator tail: edible, chicken-like meat taken from the alligator's tail, often barbecued

Bayou: a swamp

Bebop: lively jazz music

Beignet: a deep-fried French puff pastry, rolled in powdered sugar

Boogaloo: a lively rhythm and blues dance

Bourbon Street: a famous street in New Orleans, where musicians often play

Cicadas: a grasshopper-like insect

Crawfish: a freshwater crustacean that resembles a tiny lobster

Cyclone: a powerful storm or system of winds

Double Dutch: a fancy jump-rope game that uses two ropes

Doubloons: artificial Spanish coins used as party favors and thrown during Mardi Gras parades

Fat Tuesday: the Tuesday for feasting before the first fasting days of Lent

King Cake: a cake celebrating Mardi Gras that is often made with cinnamon and pecans, with a tiny plastic baby hidden and baked in it as a special surprise to be found by those eating the cake

Krewe: a special club and organization that sponsors parades or balls for Mardi Gras

Krewe of Muses: a New Orleans club, inspired by Greek mythology, whose members are all women

Kudzu: a hardy arrowroot vine that grows up to sixty feet long

Levee: a dam or wall constructed to hold back stormwater

Mardi Gras: the French term for Fat Tuesday, and a carnival celebration of the days before Lent

Lower Ninth Ward: a downriver area in New Orleans, which was the hardest hit by Katrina

Parish: another word for a small town or district

Sassafras: a spice made from the sassafras tree that is used in gumbo

St. Charles Avenue: a historic street where the Mardi Gras parades often originate

Second line: an unofficial, impromptu parade characterized by umbrellas and makeshift instruments

Shotgun house or shack: a house in which one room opens onto another room onto another room in a straight line. In New York, they are called railroad apartments

Sweet gum: a tree with star-shaped leaves often found in the South

Zulus: members of New Orleans's largest predominantly African American Mardi Gras social club, whose full name is Zulu Social Aid and Pleasure Club, Inc.